# Over in the Meadow

Illustrated by
## EZRA JACK KEATS

SCHOLASTIC BOOK SERVICES
NEW YORK · TORONTO · LONDON · AUCKLAND · SYDNEY · TOKYO

ISBN: 0-590-09195-6

Illustrations copyright © 1971 by Ezra Jack Keats. All rights reserved. Published by Scholastic Book Services, a division of Scholastic Magazines, Inc.

17 16 15 14                                          3 4 5 6/8

Printed in the U.S.A.

*To Bernice*

Over in the meadow, in the sand, in the sun,
Lived an old mother turtle and her little turtle one.

"Dig!" said the mother.
"I dig," said the one.
So he dug all day,
In the sand, in the sun.

Over in the meadow, where the stream runs blue,
Lived an old mother fish and her little fishes two.

"Swim!" said the mother.
"We swim," said the two.
So they swam and they leaped,
Where the stream runs blue.

Over in the meadow, in a hole in a tree,
Lived a mother bluebird and her little birdies three.

"Sing!" said the mother.
"We sing," said the three.
So they sang and were glad,
In the hole in the tree.

Over in the meadow, in the reeds on the shore,
Lived a mother muskrat and her little ratties four.

"Dive!" said the mother.

"We dive," said the four.

So they dived and they burrowed,

In the reeds on the shore.

Over in the meadow, in a snug beehive,
Lived a mother honeybee and her little honeys five.

"Buzz!" said the mother.

"We buzz," said the five.

So they buzzed and they hummed,

Near the snug beehive.

Over in the meadow, in a nest built of sticks,
Lived a black mother crow and her little crows six.

"Caw!" said the mother.
"We caw," said the six.
So they cawed and they called,
In their nest built of sticks.

Over in the meadow, where the grass is so even,
Lived a gay mother cricket and her little crickets seven.

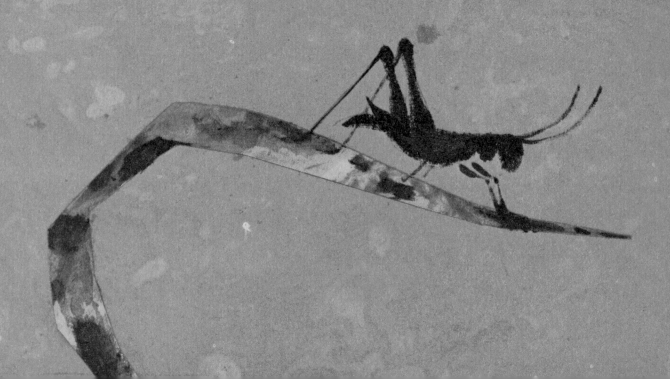

"Chirp!" said the mother.
"We chirp," said the seven.
So they chirped cheery notes,
In the grass soft and even.

Over in the meadow, by the old mossy gate,
Lived a brown mother lizard and her little lizards eight.

"Bask!" said the mother.
"We bask," said the eight.
So they basked in the sun,
By the old mossy gate.

Over in the meadow, where the clear pools shine,
Lived a green mother frog and her little froggies nine.

"Croak!" said the mother.
"We croak," said the nine.
So they croaked and they jumped,
Where the clear pools shine.

Over in the meadow, in a soft shady glen,
Lived a mother firefly and her little flies ten.

"Shine!" said the mother.
"We shine," said the ten.
So they shone like stars,
In the soft, shady glen.